PICNIC TIME

Illustrated by the Disney Storybook Artists

Published by Louis Weber, C.E.O., Publications International, Ltd., 7373 North Cicero Avenue, Lincolnwood, Illinois 60712
Ground Floor, 59 Gloucester Place, London W1U 8JJ

Customer Service: 1-800-595-8484 or customer_service@pilbooks.com

www.pilbooks.com

p i kids is a registered trademark of Publications International, Ltd.

8 7 6 5 4 3 2 1

Manufactured in China.

ISBN-13: 978-1-4508-0287-1   ISBN-10: 1-4508-0287-7

pi kids **publications international, ltd.**

It was a beautiful day at the Clubhouse. The sun shone down, and there was not a cloud in the sky.

"It's a perfect day for a picnic," Minnie said as she looked out the window.

What do you think Minnie would need in order to have a picnic?

Good food to eat? Why, sure.

Anything else?

How about good friends with whom to share the picnic?

Things for Picnic:
Tablecloth
Napkins
Plates
Fruit Salad
Lemonade
Corn on the Cob
Hot Dogs
Buns
Ketchup
Mustard

Minnie got busy making a list of all the foods and other things that her picnic would need.

Then she invited her friends to the picnic. Each friend would bring one of the foods to the picnic at noon.

Mickey
Please come
to my picnic!
Time: Today at
12 noon
Place: The Clubhouse
Playground
♡ Minnie

Goofy got his invitation at 11:30.

"Gosh," he said, "Minnie wants me to bring corn on the cob. I had better hurrry up. I only have half an hour to make it!"

Goofy boiled a pot of water. Soon the water was hot and bubbly.

Goofy counted how many members of the gang would be at the party. "Mickey, Minnie, Donald, Daisy, Pluto—and me. That makes six of us!"

Goofy cooked six ears of corn.

Daisy got her invitation at 11:45.

"Minnie wants me to bring fruit salad," Daisy said. "I only have fifteen minutes until the picnic, so I had better hurry!"

Daisy began to cut up pieces of fruit for her fruit salad.

First she cut up a pineapple.

Then she cut up melon.

Finally, she added berries to her salad.

"I think I'll make it right on time," Daisy said, proud of her fruit salad.

Donald's invitation came at 11:50.

"Oh, dear," Donald said. "Minnie wants me to make lemonade for the picnic. I only have ten minutes. I had better get going!"

Donald began to squeeze the juice from some lemons. He added sugar until it tasted sweet.

"Mmmm!" Donald said. "It tastes very good. But I bet I can make it even better."

Donald added cherries and limes to the pitcher to make a very special drink.

Mickey received his invitation right at noon. It was time for the picnic!

"It's already 12:00, Pluto," Mickey said. "Minnie's list says that we need to bring hot dogs and buns. Hot dog, we had better hurry up!"

At the grocery store, Mickey bought hot dogs, buns, ketchup, and mustard.

"A picnic wouldn't be a picnic with hot dogs," Mickey told the clerk.

Then Mickey and Pluto hurried to meet their friends.

Noon came and went and
Minnie sat all alone at the picnic
table. Where were
her friends?

Soon, she heard footsteps running toward her. And she heard the rumble of the Toon Car's engine. Her friends were on their way!

"Thank you for coming to my picnic," Minnie said.

"Sorry we were late," said Daisy.

"We just wanted to make this the best picnic ever," Mickey said.

And it really was!